Welcome Home

Aimee Reid · Rashin Kheiriyeh

Beach Lane Books

New York   London   Toronto   Sydney   New Delhi

For all the babies in our big, beautiful world
—A. R.

To all moms and dads who are expecting a baby soon, and welcome to
all newborn babies, who bring home all joy and happiness with them
من این کتاب و تقدیم میکنم به تمام پدر و مادرها و کوچولوهایی که تازه
بدنیا اومدن و با خودشان شادی را به ارمغان آوردند
—R. K.

BEACH LANE BOOKS
An imprint of Simon & Schuster Children's Publishing Division
1230 Avenue of the Americas, New York, New York 10020
Text © 2022 by Aimee Reid
Illustration © 2022 by Rashin Kheiriyeh
Book design © 2022 by Simon & Schuster, Inc.
All rights reserved, including the right of reproduction in whole or in part in any form.
BEACH LANE BOOKS and colophon are trademarks of Simon & Schuster, Inc.
For information about special discounts for bulk purchases, please contact Simon & Schuster Special Sales at
1-866-506-1949 or business@simonandschuster.com.
The Simon & Schuster Speakers Bureau can bring authors to your live event. For more information or to book an event,
contact the Simon & Schuster Speakers Bureau at 1-866-248-3049 or visit our website at www.simonspeakers.com.
The text for this book was set in Perpetua Std.
The illustrations for this book were rendered in acrylic and oil paint, pencil, ink, and oil pastel with hand-painted
papers and real feathers.
Manufactured in China
1021 SCP
First Edition
10 9 8 7 6 5 4 3 2 1
Library of Congress Cataloging-in-Publication Data
Names: Reid, Aimee, author. | Kheiriyeh, Rashin, illustrator.
Title: Welcome home / Aimee Reid ; illustrated by Rashin Kheiriyeh.
Description: First edition. | New York : Beach Lane Books, [2022] | Audience: Ages 0-8. | Audience: Grades K-1. |
Summary: Illustrations and simple, rhyming text reveal how a newborn baby is welcomed to the world by parents,
siblings, grandparents, other relatives, and neighbors.
Identifiers: LCCN 2020054056 (print) | LCCN 2020054057 (ebook) | ISBN 9781534438866 (hardcover) |
ISBN 9781534438873 (ebook)
Subjects: CYAC: Stories in rhyme. | Babies—Fiction. | Family life—Fiction. | Neighbor—Fiction.
Classification: LCC PZ8.3.R2663 Wel 2021 (print) | LCC PZ8.3.R2663 (ebook) | DDC [E]—dc23
LC record available at https://lccn.loc.gov/2020054056
LC ebook record available at https://lccn.loc.gov/2020054057

"Welcome home," says the mother,
snuggling tight
with her little one opening eyes
to the light.

"Welcome home," says the father,
quiet and clear.
Then he whispers old words
in his new baby's ear.

"Welcome home," says the brother,
smiling hello,
as he reaches to touch
just one tiny, sweet toe.

"Welcome home," say the sisters,
excited to see
the adorable baby
atop Mama's knee.

"Welcome home," says the grandma,
peaceful and wise,
as she raises her grandbaby
up to the skies.

"Welcome home," says the grandpa,
hopeful and strong,
as he wishes his grandchild
a life full and long.

"Welcome home," says the auntie,
    starting to trace
    a familiar look
        in the baby's sweet face.

"Welcome home," says the uncle,
   glowing and proud,
   the first time that he says
      the new child's name aloud.

"Welcome home," say the cousins,
hoping to play
with the new little baby
who's growing each day.

"Welcome home," say the neighbors,
gathering near,
bringing gifts and good wishes
and plenty of cheer.

"Welcome home," say the children,
circling round,
with their laughter creating
a jubilant sound.

"Welcome home, little one,
    to our blossoming lands,

to our sheltering care,
to our cradling hands."

"Welcome home," sings the mother,
tender and low,

as her heart beats a rhythm,
steady and slow.

"Welcome home to our song,
to where you belong. . . .

"Welcome to the world."